WINDOWS®
FOR BEGINNERS

Richard Dungworth

Edited by Philippa Wingate

Editorial consultants: Jane Chisholm & Anthony Marks

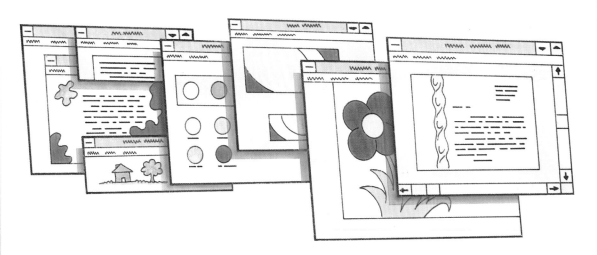

Designed by Neil Francis & Steve Page

Additional designs by Sarah Bealham, Non Figg & Russell Punter

Illustrated by Colin Mier, Derek Matthews, Andy Burton, Pete Taylor and Paul Southcombe

Technical Consultant: Richard Payne

Contents

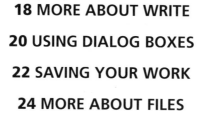

Introducing Microsoft Windows

You can use your personal computer, or PC, for all sorts of amazing jobs. But before it can perform even the simplest task, your PC needs a list of instructions, called a program. To make sure that your computer has all the instructions it needs, you can buy whole sets of programs, grouped together as software.

Your computer needs software before it can work.

What is Microsoft Windows?

Microsoft® Windows® is a special piece of software which enables you to tell your PC what you want it to do. You use Windows to control all the other software on your computer. This section of the book explains the simple techniques you'll need to become one of the 80 million people who use Windows to control their PC.

Windows lets you control your PC quickly and easily.

Windows versions

From time to time Microsoft brings out a new version of the Windows system. The new version includes various improvements on earlier versions. Each Windows version is given a number. The higher the number, the more recent the version.

This section of the book concentrates on version 3.1 of the Windows software. Its screen pictures show the Windows® 3.1 display. But you can use the same techniques to operate other versions of Windows, including Windows® 3.11.

Windows 95

The most advanced version of Microsoft Windows is called Windows® 95. You can find out more about the Windows® 95 system on pages 46 & 47.

About this section

This section of the book introduces all the main features of Windows, telling you how to use them step-by-step. The first time you read it, work through page by page from beginning to end. Later, you can use the index at the back of the book to look up particular topics to refresh your memory.

Getting help

Some pages include "help" boxes with a lifebelt in the top left-hand corner. These boxes contain tips to help you cope as you find your way around Windows.

If you need extra help, you can find out on pages 44 and 45 how to use the instructions that are included in the Windows software.

DOS, Windows and applications

In order to work properly, a computer needs a piece of software called an operating system. One of an operating system's main jobs is to take in commands from the person using the computer (known as the user) and convert them into instructions which the computer can understand.

MS-DOS

Most personal computers use an operating system called Microsoft Disk Operating System. It is known as MS-DOS or DOS for short. With DOS, you tell your computer what to do by typing in command codes using your PC's keyboard. Some DOS commands are rather complicated.

To make DOS easier to use, Microsoft developed the Windows system. Windows works with DOS to enable you to control your computer without having to type in DOS commands.

How does Windows work?

The Windows system fills your PC's display with pictures. By "touching" or moving these pictures in a particular way, using an on-screen pointer, you can tell Windows what you want your computer to do. Windows then controls DOS on your behalf to make your computer carry out your commands.

This screen shows the Windows display.

You will find out about the different pictures which make up the Windows display on pages 8 and 9.

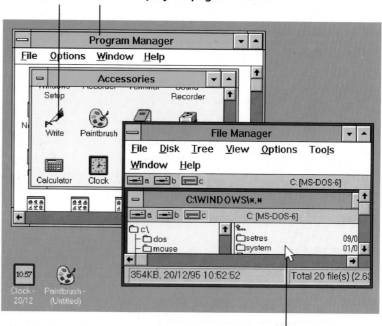

This pointer enables you to touch specific parts of the display.

Mouse control

Instead of using your computer's keyboard to control the Windows pointer, you move it around using a hand-held device, connected to the computer by a thin cable. Because of its shape and its cable "tail", this gadget is known as a mouse.

You will find out how to use your computer's mouse on pages 10 and 11 of this book.

4

Application software

Windows enables your PC to use, or "run", other pieces of software, called applications. Each application includes the instructions and information that your computer needs to play a particular role.

You can buy applications for a remarkable range of jobs. Games, drawing programs, and so-called spreadsheets and databases are all examples of applications. The picture below shows some of the things you can do with your PC by running applications.

Work with text

Produce film

Make music

Draw and design

Compatibility

When you buy an application to use with Windows on your PC, you must make sure that it is designed to be controlled with Windows, rather than with another operating system. Applications which work with the Windows system are said to be Windows compatible.

What you need to begin

To use Windows, you need a PC which can run the Windows software. Windows and its applications were originally designed for use on computers built by a company called IBM. But many other companies now sell PCs which are "IBM compatible", and can use the Windows system.

Some computers which run Windows are small enough to fit on your lap.

Installing Windows

Most PCs already have DOS and Windows software when you buy them. If yours doesn't, you need to buy the software and feed it into your PC. This is known as installing the software. Follow the installation instructions that are included with the software.

Standard applications

The applications used in this book to introduce Windows techniques are included in the Windows software when you buy it. So you don't need to buy any extra software to start learning.

You will find out on pages 16-21 how to use an application called Write to create a letter to a friend.

Pages 26-29 explain how you can use the Paintbrush application to draw pictures.

Starting and stopping

Before you can use Windows, you need to switch on your computer, and start the Windows software running.

Switching on

To switch on your computer, press its power switch. You also need to switch on the piece of equipment that shows your PC's display, called a monitor. Some monitors automatically come on when the computer that they're connected to is switched on, but others have a separate on/off switch.

Your computer will begin to make whirring noises. Long lists of command codes will begin to scroll up your screen. If this doesn't happen, check that all the power leads are plugged in properly, and that the electricity is switched on at the socket.

WARNING!
Electricity from the mains socket can be very dangerous. Never fiddle with plugs when the mains switch is on.

Running Windows

Once your computer is switched on, you need to make sure that the Windows software is running. Most computers which use Windows either automatically run the Windows software as they are switched on, or start up in DOS (see page 4).

If your PC is set to run the Windows software automatically, your screen will briefly show a picture of a multicoloured flag (the Windows logo) before filling with the Windows display.

If your computer starts in DOS, the "DOS prompt", shown below, will appear on your screen.

The DOS prompt

In this case you need to start Windows running yourself. Type the letters WIN and press the **Return** key. The Windows logo and display will then appear on your screen.

Keystroke commands

As you work through this book, you will occasionally need to use your computer's keyboard to enter a command. This is known as using keystrokes. The keystrokes included in this book are printed in bold type, **like this**. Although keyboards vary, the diagram below should help you find the keys you need.

This diagram shows the typical layout of a PC's keyboard.

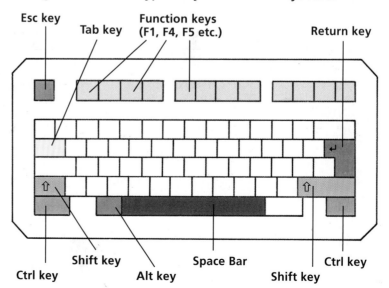

Computer health

Once you have successfully started Windows running, you can find out how to use it by working through the rest of this book. However, long periods of computing may damage your health. So, as you work with your PC, it is important to take a break at least once an hour. When you take a short break, you can leave your computer switched on.

Screen savers

Don't be alarmed if you return after a break to find an unusual screen display. A monitor's screen can be damaged by showing the same image for a long time. So Windows often puts a moving "screen saver" on display if your mouse and keyboard are left untouched for a while.

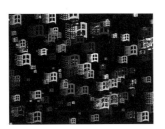

The Windows display will return as soon as you give your mouse a nudge.

This screen shows an example of a Windows screen saver.

HELP!

When you disturb a screen saver, a box like the one below may appear on your screen. This means that the screen saver is "locked" on. To return to the Windows display you will need to ask the person who set this lock for their screen saver password.

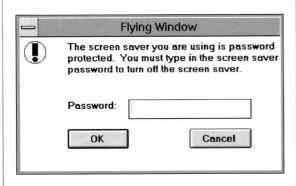

Shutting down

Another important thing to know is how to stop when you've finished using Windows for the day. This is known as shutting down.

Before you switch off your PC's power supply, you must bring your Windows session to an end. Switching off the power while Windows is still running can damage your computer.

Ending your session

When you are ready to shut down, follow the steps below to bring your Windows session to an end:

1 - Make sure that you have selected the part of the Windows system called Program Manager. You will find out how to do this on page 9.

2 - While holding down the **Alt** key, press the **F4** key. Release both keys.

3 - The box shown below will appear on your screen. If you have changed your mind about stopping, press and release the **Esc** key. Otherwise press and release the **Return** key.

As Windows stops running, its display will vanish from the screen, and your computer will return to DOS. Once the DOS prompt appears, you can safely switch off your PC and its monitor.

The Windows desktop

Once Windows is running, it fills your screen with a display called the desktop. Your desktop may be almost empty to begin with, but as you work with Windows, it will become crowded with pictures, like the example shown on the right. These pages introduce the main parts of the Windows desktop.

This screen shows a crowded Windows desktop.

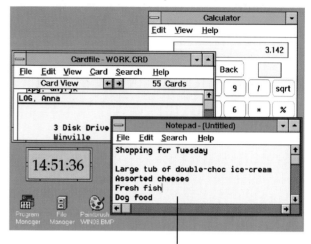

Programs and pictures

Just like an ordinary desk, a busy Windows desktop is scattered with useful items. But instead of providing a real notepad, calculator, address book, or clock, Windows spreads out programs that do the same jobs as these articles. Each picture on the desktop represents one of these programs. There are two main types of desktop picture, called windows and icons.

When an item on the Windows desktop overlaps others, it is described as being nearer the top of the desktop.

What is a window?

A window is a rectangular box, with a thin border on all four sides, and a thicker strip across its top edge. The picture below shows what a typical window looks like, and what its various parts are called. You will find out on pages 12 and 13 what a window's borders, buttons and bars are for.

A window

This small square with a slot in is called a control-menu box.

This strip across the top edge of a window is called a title bar.

Most windows have a second strip containing a row of words. This is called a menu bar.

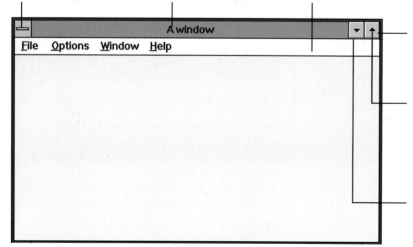

The top right-hand corner of each window contains two small squares which look like buttons.

This button can appear in two forms. If it shows a single upward pointing arrow it is called a maximize button. But if it shows a double-arrow like this, it is called a restore button.

This button, showing a downward pointing arrow, is called a minimize button.

Icons

Instead of appearing as a window, a program can be represented on the desktop by a small picture, called an icon. Icons can appear anywhere on your desktop. They are often found along the bottom edge of your screen.

An icon usually has a label underneath it, giving the name of the program it represents.

These are some of the icons that you will come across on your Windows desktop.

File Manager   Paintbrush   Clock   Calculator

Write   Notepad   Cardfile   Calendar

The appearance of a program's icon often provides a clue to what that program is for. For example, the icon for Paintbrush, a program which lets you draw pictures, looks like an artist's paint palette and brush.

The pointer

Somewhere on your desktop you'll find the pointer (see page 4). The pointer usually appears as a small arrowhead, but depending on what you are using it for, it can take on any of the forms shown below.

The arrowhead pointer

Other pointer shapes

Wallpaper

The Windows desktop is sometimes decorated with a patterned layer, called wallpaper. There are lots of different designs of desktop wallpaper.

This screen shows an example of Windows wallpaper.

Finding Program Manager

On the next two pages of this book you will find out how to use your mouse to control the Windows desktop. You'll use a window called Program Manager for this mouse practice, so you need to make sure that the Program Manager window is on top of your desktop.

Hold down the **Alt** key. When you press and release the **Tab** key, a box containing an icon and its name will appear in the middle of your screen. If the icon and name are different from those shown in the box below, keep the **Alt** key held down and press and release the **Tab** key again. Keep doing this until the box shows Program Manager's icon and name as shown below.

 Program Manager

Now release the **Alt** key and Program Manager's window will jump to the top of your desktop. To make sure the window fills your screen, hold down the **Alt** key and press the **Space Bar**. Release both keys, and type the letter **X**.

You'll find out more about Program Manager on pages 14 and 15.

Using your mouse

Now that you know what the Windows desktop looks like, you can find out how to use it to tell your computer what to do.

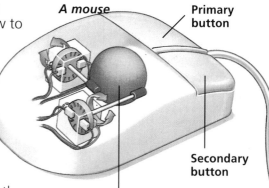

A mouse — **Primary button**

Secondary button

As you move the mouse, the motion of this ball is converted into movement of the pointer across your screen.

Pointing things out

To operate the desktop, you use the on-screen pointer as an electronic finger to pick out and move around specific parts of the display. You control the pointer's movements using a mouse (see page 4). The picture on the right shows a computer mouse, cut away so that you can see inside.

Most mice have two switches on their top surface, called the primary and secondary mouse buttons. The primary button is usually on the left, as shown in the picture. But if your computer is set for a left-handed mouse user, the buttons swap positions.

Mouse movements

Try moving your mouse about on a flat, clean surface. The pointer will follow your mouse movements by moving across the screen.

This is how you hold your mouse.

Use a special mouse mat if you have one, but a hardback book or a clear area of desk will do.

If your mouse reaches the edge of the surface that you're using it on, lift it up and replace it near the middle of the surface. By lifting your mouse, you can reposition it on your work surface without altering the position of the pointer on your screen. Use this technique to make the space you need to move your mouse in the direction you want.

Clicking

To "touch" part of the display, use your mouse to move the pointer over it, and then press and release the primary mouse button (see above). This is called clicking. It is the main way in which you use your mouse to control Windows.

You can click on various bits of the desktop, some of which look like buttons. Have a go at clicking on the restore button in the top right-hand corner of Program Manager's window on your screen (see page 8). Clicking on this button will cause the window to shrink so that it covers only part of the desktop, rather than filling the whole screen.

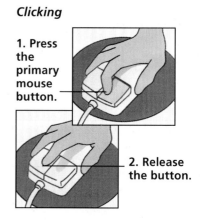

Clicking

1. Press the primary mouse button.

2. Release the button.

'Click' 'Click' 'Click'

Dragging

To move something around on the desktop, you use another mouse technique, called dragging.

Position the pointer over the item you want to move. Press and hold down the primary mouse button. Imagine that you are grabbing and holding on to the item. By keeping the primary button depressed as you move your mouse, you can drag the item to another area of the desktop. Once it is where you want it, release the mouse button to drop the item into its new desktop location.

Try out your dragging technique by moving the Program Manager window to a new position on your desktop. To move the window, drag its title bar.

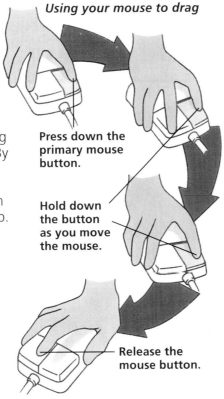

Using your mouse to drag

Press down the primary mouse button.

Hold down the button as you move the mouse.

Release the mouse button.

Double-clicking

The final mouse technique is called double-clicking. This is a special way of touching an item on the desktop. To double-click on part of your display, move the pointer over it and press and release the primary mouse button twice in quick succession.

Double-clicking usually offers a shortcut way to do something. For example, double-clicking on a window's title bar provides a speedy way to change the window's size. Try out your double-click on the Program Manager window's title bar.

Mouse lessons

To improve your mouse skills, you can use a lesson which is included in the Windows software. This is how you start the lesson:

1 - Make sure that the Program Manager window is selected (see page 9).

2 - While holding down the **Alt** key, type the letter **H**. Release both keys.

3 - Type the letter **W**.

Now follow the instructions which appear on your screen to use the Mouse Lesson. When you have had enough mouse practice, press the **Esc** key to return to the desktop display.

'Click' 'Click'

HELP!

If you lose sight of Program Manager as you try out your mouse skills, you can bring it back to the top of your desktop using the **Alt** and **Tab** keys (see page 9). You'll find out more about how to find things on your Windows desktop on pages 40 & 41.

Controlling a window

A window provides a workspace on your desktop in which you can use a particular program. Now that you can click, drag and double-click, you need to know how to use these mouse skills to control a typical window, so that you can work with Windows programs.

Open windows

Windows that appear on your desktop are said to be open. Your computer can run several programs at the same time, so several windows can be open on the desktop. However, you can only use one of these open windows at a time.

Active or inactive?

When a particular window is in use it is known as the active window. It lies on top of the other "inactive" windows on your desktop, and usually has a different coloured title bar.

When you want to use a specific window, you can make it active by clicking on any part of it. If you can't do this because the window is hidden by other items on your desktop, you will need to use one of the techniques described on pages 40 and 41 to "switch" to the window that you want to use.

A busy desktop

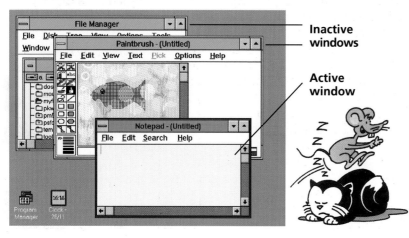

Inactive windows

Active window

Minimizing

If your desktop gets crowded with open windows, you can make some space by reducing the amount of room taken up by windows that you're not currently working with. By clicking on the minimize button in the top right-hand corner of a window, you can reduce that window to an icon at the bottom of your screen. This is known as minimizing a window.

Minimizing lets you put a program to one side for the time being. If you want to use that program again, you can convert its icon back into a window by double-clicking on it. Returning a window to its original size and location on your desktop is known as restoring that window.

Minimizing and restoring

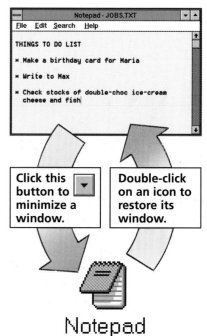

Click this button to minimize a window.

Double-click on an icon to restore its window.

Notepad

Maximizing

If you want more space inside a particular window, you can expand it so that it fills your screen. To do this, click on the window's maximize button.

A window which has been maximized fills the entire screen and has no surrounding border. Instead of a maximize button it has a restore button. You can return the window to its previous size and position by clicking this restore button.

Maximizing and restoring

Click this button to maximize a window.

Click this button to restore a window.

Changing a window's size

You can adjust the size of a window, stretching or shrinking it to make it wider, narrower, taller or shorter. To alter a window's size, point to the border that you want to move. The pointer will change into a double-headed arrow, showing the directions in which you can alter the window's shape. Hold down the mouse button and drag the border to a new position.

This diagram shows you the different ways in which you can change a window's size.

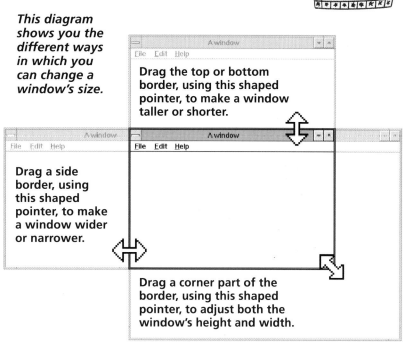

Drag the top or bottom border, using this shaped pointer, to make a window taller or shorter.

Drag a side border, using this shaped pointer, to make a window wider or narrower.

Drag a corner part of the border, using this shaped pointer, to adjust both the window's height and width.

Moving a window

Unless it has been maximized to fill the screen, you can move a window around the desktop by dragging its title bar to a new location.

Using scroll bars

Sometimes a window isn't big enough to display all its contents. When this is the case, the window has a "scroll bar" along its right edge, its bottom edge, or both these edges. You can use these scroll bars to shift the window's view so that you can look at any part of its contents.

To move your view a little at a time, click on the arrow button at either end of a scroll bar. To shift your view by a whole window size, click on the scroll bar itself. Or you can drag the small square called the scroll box along the scroll bar until the window shows the area you want.

A window with scroll bars

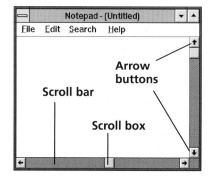

Arrow buttons

Scroll bar

Scroll box

Program Manager

To use a Windows program, you need to open its window on your desktop by running that program.

These pages introduce Program Manager, the part of the Windows system that lets you find and run the programs that you need. To explore Program Manager, make sure that its window is active and maximized (see pages 12 and 13).

Tidying the display

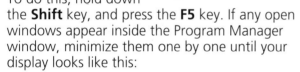

When you use the Program Manager window for the first time, it's a good idea to tidy up your display, so that you can see where everything is. To do this, hold down the **Shift** key, and press the **F5** key. If any open windows appear inside the Program Manager window, minimize them one by one until your display looks like this:

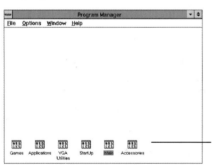

Several icons will line up along the bottom of the Program Manager window.

Program group icons

Program Manager gathers all the programs on your computer into "program groups". Each program group has its own name, and is represented by a "program group icon" inside the Program Manager window.

A program group icon

Each icon is labelled with the name of the group it represents.

Program group windows

To find out which programs a particular program group contains, double-click on its program group icon. A window will appear inside the Program Manager window. This type of window is called a program group window. Once a program group window is open, it displays an icon for each of the programs included in that group.

This screen shows the Accessories program group window open inside Program Manager's window.

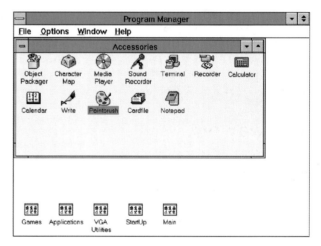

Finding a program

To run a program that you want to use, you need to find the icon that represents that program. To do this, use Program Manager to open and search each program group window until you find the icon you need. You may have to use scroll bars on a program group window to search its contents thoroughly.

Each time you open a program group window, use the **Shift** and **F5** keys to tidy up the Program Manager window. If Program Manager becomes cluttered with open program group windows, make some space by minimizing the ones you are not using. This will change them back into program group icons.

Running a program

Once you have found the icon for the program you want, you can start the program running. To do this, you simply double-click on the program's icon.

As a program starts running, its window appears on top of your desktop. The program will remain on your desktop, as a window or an icon, until you stop it running. On page 25 you'll find out how to stop a program running by "closing" its window.

The way out

The Program Manager window also enables you to bring your Windows session to an end. You found out on page 7 how to stop Windows running by using keystrokes to close the Program Manager window.

Once you've learned how to use clicking to close a window (see page 25) you'll be able to use your mouse, rather than the keyboard, to close Program Manager and quit Windows.

EXIT

Using menu commands

Like most other windows, the Program Manager window has a menu bar containing several words. When you click on one of the words in a window's menu bar, a list of possible commands called a menu drops down beneath that word. You can select one of these commands by clicking on it.

Some menus include shortcut keystrokes for certain commands. You can use these as an alternative to using your mouse to enter the command.

Choosing commands from menus is one of the main ways in which you use Windows to control your PC.

Window	
Cascade	Shift+F5
Tile	Shift+F4
Arrange Icons	
1 Main	
2 Applications	
3 Accessories	
4 Games	
5 Start Up	

Try using Program Manager's Window menu, shown here, to open a particular program group window.

This keyboard short cut means "hold down the Shift key and press the F4 key".

Disabled menu commands

Some of the commands included in a menu may appear in faded text. These are known as disabled commands. Clicking on a disabled menu command has no effect.

Other parts of the Windows display, such as command buttons, can also appear in disabled form.

This menu includes two disabled commands.

Disabled buttons like these won't respond to clicking.

File	
New...	
Open	Enter
Move...	F7
Copy...	F8
Delete	Del
Properties...	Alt+Enter
Run...	
Exit Windows...	

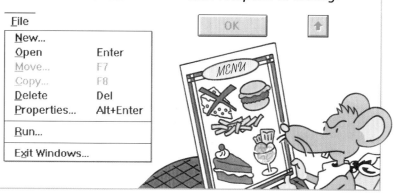

Word processing with Write

Now that you know how to find and run a program, you can try out a Windows application. Use Program Manager to find the icon for a program called Write. It looks like this, and is usually found in the Accessories program group. Double-click on the Write icon to set the Write application running.

What is Write?

Write is an application which enables you to work with text. Text is made up of individual units called characters, which can be letters of the alphabet, numbers, punctuation marks, symbols or even spaces. Write lets you type text into your computer and then organize it to form a document such as a letter or story. This kind of application is called a word processing program.

The Write window

As you start Write running, its window appears on your desktop. This window provides all the tools you will need to create a text document. The area inside the window displays your Write document, which starts off as a blank page. Maximize the Write window to take a closer look at its various parts.

This screen shows the Write window in maximized form. The top left-hand corner is magnified so that you can see it more clearly.

The title bar displays the name of your document ("untitled" at this point).

The menu bar is used to enter your commands (see page 15).

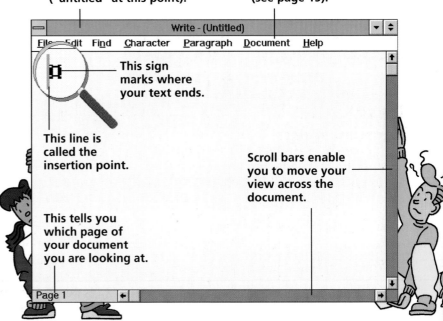

This sign marks where your text ends.

This line is called the insertion point.

Scroll bars enable you to move your view across the document.

This tells you which page of your document you are looking at.

Entering text

The flashing vertical line inside Write's page area is called the insertion point. It shows you where your text will be placed on the page when you start typing. Try it out by typing in the words "Word processing with Write". As you type, the text will appear to the left of the insertion point, as shown below.

—	Write - (l
File Edit Find Character Parac

Word processing with Write

The I-beam

When you point inside Write's page area, the pointer turns into a tall "I" shape. This special pointer is called the I-beam. You use it to position the insertion point anywhere within your document.

Using your mouse, move the I-beam to the left of the word "with". Click the primary mouse button, and the insertion point will jump to this new location. Now type the words "is easy". This new text will insert itself in your document to the left of the insertion point's new position.

Deleting text

To rub out, or "delete", some of your text, use the I-beam to place the insertion point to the right of the text you want to remove. Press the **Backspace** key to delete one character at a time. The **Backspace** key usually has an arrow on it, pointing to the left. On most keyboards it is found above the **Return** key (see page 6).

Try deleting the words "with Write" that you typed onto your Write page earlier.

The Backspace key

Selecting text

You can also use the I-beam to mark out parts of your document that you want to alter. This is called selecting. To select a section of text, move the I-beam to the left of the first character in that section. Holding down the mouse button, drag the I-beam until it is just to the right of the last character in the section. When you release the mouse button, the selected text remains highlighted, as shown below.

Highlighted Write text looks like this

Deleting a block

You can delete a chunk of text, known as a text "block", by selecting it and pressing the **Backspace** key. All the highlighted text will be removed from your document. Try deleting the remaining words on your Write page in this way.

Shortcut selecting

There are several speedy ways to select parts of your document. To select an individual word, simply double-click the I-beam on it. To select an entire line of text, click in the left-hand margin next to that line with the arrow-shaped pointer, or hold down the **Ctrl** key and click the I-beam somewhere along the line. To select your entire document, hold down the **Ctrl** key and click in the left-hand margin with the arrow-shaped pointer.

WARNING!

While a block of text is selected, any new text that you type in will replace it. To avoid this happening accidentally, you should "deselect" a block of text once you have finished altering it. Click the insertion point somewhere else in your document. The text will be deselected, losing its highlighting.

Writing with Write

You can use what you have learned on these pages to type in a letter to one of your friends. Write will automatically start a new line each time you reach the right-hand margin. If you want to start a new line before you reach the right-hand margin, press the **Return** key. Use the selection and insertion techniques to correct any mistakes you make as you go along.

More about Write

Once you have typed your text onto a Write page, you can change it until it is just the way you want. Altering a document like this is called editing.

Choosing a style

Write's *Character* menu provides a variety of options for editing the appearance of your text. For example, you can choose from several text styles. To do this, select the text that you want to alter, then click on one of the *Character* menu commands shown in the chart below.

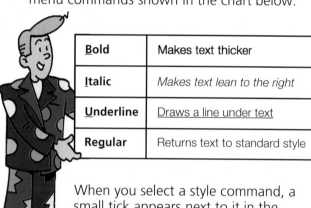

Bold	Makes text thicker
Italic	*Makes text lean to the right*
Underline	<u>Draws a line under text</u>
Regular	Returns text to standard style

When you select a style command, a small tick appears next to it in the *Character* menu. If you click on a style command with a tick next to it, the tick disappears, and the style is switched off. You can combine text styles by picking more than one style command.

√ **Bold**	**Ctrl+B**	
√ *Italic*	**Ctrl+I**	
√ <u>Underline</u>	**Ctrl+U**	

See what your text looks like when you combine these three styles.

Sizing your text

The *Character* menu also lets you alter the size of your text. To do this, first select the text you want to resize. If you want to make this text smaller, click on the *Reduce Font* command. To make it larger, click on the *Enlarge Font* command.

Enlarge or reduce?

The Paragraph menu

As well as altering the style and size of your text, you can choose how you want it to be positioned on your page. The borders that surround the text are called margins. By selecting a block of text, and then clicking on a command in Write's *Paragraph* menu, you can place the text in different positions between the left and right margins, as shown below.

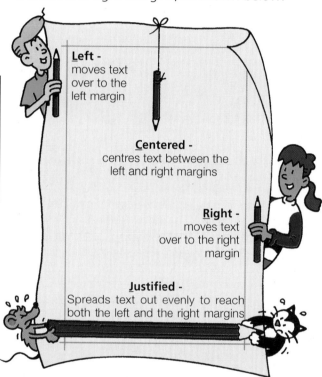

Left - moves text over to the left margin

Centered - centres text between the left and right margins

Right - moves text over to the right margin

Justified - Spreads text out evenly to reach both the left and the right margins

Spacing out your text

You can also use Write's *Paragraph* menu to choose how much space there is between one line of your text and the next. Select the text block whose line-spacing you want to alter, and choose from the *Single Space*, *1½ Space*, or *Double Space* commands in the *Paragraph* menu.

Parting is such sweet sorrow

To return text to Write's standard layout (single spaced text, aligned to the left margin), select the text and click on the *Normal* command in the *Paragraph* menu.

The ruler

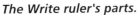

Instead of using menu commands, you can edit your Write document using the "ruler" If you pick the *Ruler On* option from Write's *Document* menu, a horizontal ruler appears across the top edge of the Write window.

Each of the ruler's boxes and bits performs the same function as one of Write's menu commands. Select the text you want to alter, and click on the part of the ruler which creates the effect you want.

The Write ruler's parts.

Clicking on one of these boxes sets the spacing between one text line and the next.

Clicking this box moves selected text over to the left margin.

Clicking this box positions text centrally between the side margins.

Clicking this box moves selected text over to the right margin.

Clicking this box spreads selected text evenly between the left and right margins.

Using the Clipboard

You can move a block of text from one place in your document to another using the Windows Clipboard system. Select the text that you want to move. Pick *Cut* from Write's *Edit* menu. The text will be removed from your document and be placed out of sight on the Clipboard. Using the I-beam, move the insertion point to the text's new location. Pick *Paste* from the *Edit* menu and the text will be copied from the Clipboard back into your document.

1. Select the text you want to move and pick Cut.

The selected text is placed on the Clipboard.

2. Move the insertion point to the text's new location.

3. Pick Paste.

The text is copied back into your document.

Copying your text

If you select a block of text and pick the *Copy* command from Write's *Edit* menu, the text will be copied onto your Clipboard without being removed from its original location. You can then use the insertion point and the *Paste* command to insert the copied text in other places in your document.

WARNING!
The Clipboard can hold only one chunk of information at a time. Cutting or copying something new onto the Clipboard deletes whatever was previously there.

Clipboard Viewer

If you want to find out what is currently stored on your Clipboard, you can use Program Manager to find and run a program called Clipboard Viewer. This displays the contents of the Clipboard inside a window on your desktop.

The Clipboard Viewer icon

Using dialog boxes

As you use a Windows application, you will come across some menu commands which end in three dots. Whenever you pick one of these commands, Windows displays a questionnaire called a dialog box on your desktop. Dialog boxes let you enter information about what you want to do.

Fonts

An example of a Windows dialog box is the one you use in Write to choose a "font". A font is a complete set of letters, numbers and symbols of a particular appearance. As you create a document, you can choose from a range of fonts, to make your text look just the way you want. Each font has its own name.

This picture shows a selection of the many different text fonts.

Write's Font box

You can pick a font before you type in your Write text, or select a block of existing text and change it to a particular font. In either case, you use a dialog box to enter your choice of font. Click on the *Fonts...* option in Write's *Character* menu. After a brief pause, Write's Font dialog box will appear on your desktop.

This is Write's Font dialog box.

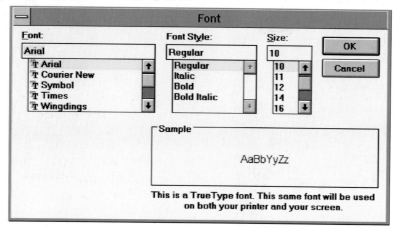

Changing settings

Three smaller boxes inside the Font dialog box display the current text settings. They show the name of the font, and the style and size of the text (see page 18).

By scrolling through the list of possible settings beneath each of these three boxes, and clicking on a font, style and size of your choice, you can enter new text settings.

A sample of text in the font, style and size that you have specified appears in the Sample box at the bottom right-hand corner of the Font dialog box. If you are happy with your choices, click the *OK* button. The dialog box will disappear, and your new text settings will take effect.

Dialog controls

Write's Font box is one of the many different dialog boxes you will encounter as you use the Windows system. Some contain special gadgets, such as buttons, boxes or lists. You use each of these gadgets in a particular way to enter information.

This pretend pizza order form gives you an idea of how some of the common dialog box controls work.

This is an OPTION BUTTON. Click on it to select one of several options. A dot appears inside the circle next to the selected option.

You can click on these up and down arrows to make a number setting larger or smaller.

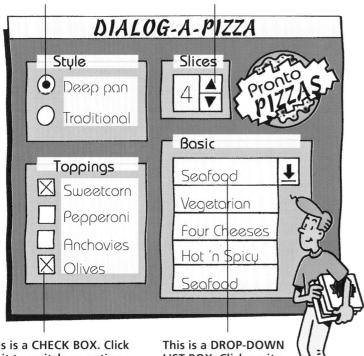

This is a CHECK BOX. Click on it to switch an option on or off. If an option is on, a cross appears in its box. You can select more than one check box option.

This is a DROP-DOWN LIST BOX. Click on its arrow button to open a list of options. You can then select one option by clicking on it.

HELP!

To try out the various dialog box gadgets, you can follow the section on dialog boxes in the Windows Tutorial. Find out how to follow a particular section of the Windows Tutorial on page 45.

OK or Cancel?

When you have selected new settings in a dialog box, you make your choices take effect by clicking on the box's *OK* button.

If you decide that you don't want to make the changes you have selected after all, you can abandon a dialog box by clicking on its *Cancel* button. The dialog box will vanish from the desktop, and your document will remain unchanged.

Writing with Write

Use what you now know about Write's controls and commands to edit the letter that you typed in on page 17. Try aligning your address to the right margin. You could alter the font, style and size of parts of your text, or even use the Clipboard to rearrange the order of your letter.

Whoops!

Write's *Edit* menu includes a command called *Undo*. Whenever you use the ruler, menu commands, the Clipboard or dialog boxes to edit your text, and then regret it, click on *Undo* to cancel your last editing step. Most Windows applications have an *Undo* command.

Saving your work

When you have produced a document using an application, Windows lets you store it away so that you can return to it later. This is known as saving your work.

Disks, drives and files

Inside your computer is a device called a hard disk, which can store lots of information. The hard disk sits inside a hard disk drive, which records information onto it.

Your computer stores each batch of information, such as a Write document, as a "file" on the hard disk. When you want to use a particular piece of information again, the hard disk drive retrieves the file you need.

Floppies

A floppy disk is a small disk, cased in plastic, which can store files in much the same way as a hard disk. You insert a "floppy" into its disk drive through a slot in your computer.

If you save a file on a floppy disk, you can remove the disk from its drive and take the file away to use on another computer.

This cutaway picture of a PC shows the main types of disk drive.

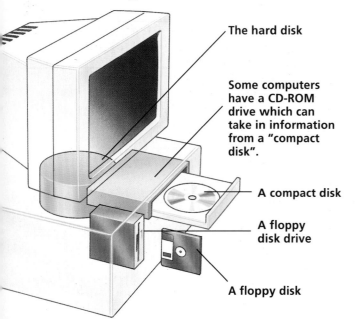

The hard disk

Some computers have a CD-ROM drive which can take in information from a "compact disk".

A compact disk

A floppy disk drive

A floppy disk

The Save As box

Before you can save a document as a file on disk, you need to give it a name, and tell the computer where on disk you want to keep it. Windows applications have a dialog box, called a Save As box, which lets you enter these details when you save a document.

To find out how to use a Save As box, try saving the Write letter that you created on the previous pages. Pick the *Save As...* command from Write's *File* menu. The dialog box below will appear on your desktop:

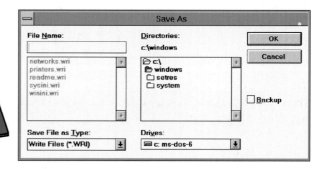

Naming your file

To give your Write letter a name, click the insertion point into the box labelled "File Name" in the top left-hand corner of Write's Save As box. Then type in the name of your choice. You can give a Windows file a name that is up to eight characters long. It cannot include spaces, or any of the characters shown below:

. : / \ [ ] * | < > + = ; , ?

A filename is usually followed by something called an extension. This consists of a full stop and a three character code. Each application has its own filename extension. Your computer can tell from an extension what type of file it is dealing with. Add the extension ".wri" to your filename to label your file as a Write document.

The File Name box

File **Name**:

`maria.wri`

You could use your name or initials as a filename.

Picking a drive

The next step when saving a file is to choose the disk drive that holds the disk on which you want to store your file.

Near the bottom of the Save As box is a box labelled "Drives". Click on the Drives box to see a drop-down list of all your PC's disk drives.

The Drives box

Drives:

⊟ c: ms-dos-6	±
⊟ a:	
⊟ b:	
⊟ c: ms-dos-6	

Each of your computer's drives is represented in the Drives box by a symbol labelled with a letter.

To save your Write letter on the hard disk, pick the hard disk drive by clicking on it in the Drives list. It is represented by this symbol, and is usually labelled as the "c" drive.

Directories

You can gather the files stored on a disk into groups. This is rather like organizing lots of paper documents into separate folders. It makes it easier to find a specific file later on. The "folders" on a disk are called directories.

The disk on which you are about to save your file may contain several directories, so you need to specify which one you want to store your file in before you can save it. Above the Drives box in the Save As dialog box is a box labelled "Directories". This displays a list of all the directories on the disk in the drive that you've selected. Each one is represented by a small folder symbol, labelled with a directory name.

Picking a directory

To save your file in a particular directory, you need to find that directory's folder symbol in the Directories list and double-click on it.

You will find out on page 34 how to create a personal directory in which to keep your own work. In the meantime you should save your Write letter in the main directory on the hard disk, known as the hard disk root directory (see page 31). To open this directory, double-click on the folder symbol labelled "c:\" at the top of the Directories list.

The Directories box

Directories:

c:\

📂 c:\	↑
📁 dos	
📁 mouse	
📁 temp	
📁 windows	↓

Giving the OK

You have now told your computer what you want to call your file and where you want to store it. Click on the Save As box's *OK* button, and your computer will save your document. The Save As dialog box will disappear, and your document's filename will appear across the title bar of the Write window. A copy of your letter is now safely stored as a file in the root directory on the hard disk.

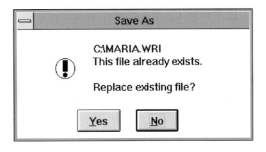

HELP!

This box may appear on your screen when you try to save your document. This means that the directory you've picked already contains a file with the name that you've chosen. Click the *No* button, use the Save As box to give your file a different name, and try the *OK* button again.

Save As
C:\MARIA.WRI ⓘ This file already exists. Replace existing file? [Yes]   [No]

More about files

On these pages, you will find out how to retrieve a Windows file from disk when you want to use it. You will also learn how to keep your files up to date.

The Open box

Retrieving a file from disk is known as opening a file. To enable you to find and open any file previously created using an application, Windows provides a special dialog box, called an Open box.

Have a go at opening the file that you saved on page 23. Make sure that Write's window is open and active. If it still contains your letter, pick the *New* command from the *File* menu to clear away this document, so that you can try retrieving it from disk. Click on the *Open...* command in the Write window's *File* menu. Write's Open box will appear on your desktop.

Write's Open box.

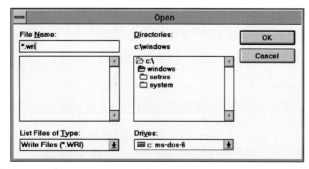

Opening a directory

You use an Open box to tell your computer the name of the file you want to open, and where to find it. Your Write letter file is stored in the root directory on your PC's hard disk (see page 23). Use the "Drives" list inside Write's Open box to pick the hard disk drive. Then use the "Directories" list to open up the root directory, just as you did on page 23.

Selecting a file

Once you have opened a directory, a list of filenames appears in the left-hand part of the Open box. This is an alphabetical list of all the files in the open directory that match the application you are using. Because you are using Write's Open box, the list will show all the files in the directory that end in ".wri".

Scroll through the list of filenames until you find the one you want. By clicking on your letter's filename, you can enter it into the "File Name" box at the top of the list.

Now that you've told your computer which file you want to open, and where to find it, click on the *OK* button. Your PC will retrieve the file from disk. The Open box will vanish, and your letter will appear in the Write window.

The File Name box

File Name:

| maria.wri |

| maria.wri | ↑ |
| | ↓ |

The Save option

If you alter a document after you've retrieved it from disk, you may want to save the new version.

There is no need to use the Save As box, as you did on page 22, to save the new version of your document. Your file already has a name and disk location. Instead you can simply click on the *Save* command in the *File* menu. Your computer will automatically store the latest version of your document in its original disk location, under its original filename.

Keeping up to date

As you work on a Windows document, you should use the *Save* command regularly to keep the version on disk "updated". This means that if your PC's power supply fails for any reason, you will be able to retrieve the most recent version of your document from disk.

WARNING!
When you use the *Save* command, your PC replaces the previous version of your document on disk with the new version.

If you want to keep both versions of a document, you need to save the new version as a separate file, using the *Save As...* command to give it a different filename. One way of naming a new version of a document is to add a number to the original document's filename.

Closing a window

To stop a Windows program running, you have to close its window. To do this you click on the control-menu box in the top left-hand corner of the window (see page 8).

The window's "control menu" will appear. Pick the *Close* command from this control menu. As a speedy alternative, you can close a window simply by double-clicking on its control-menu box.

When you have finished your Write letter, and saved the latest version of it on disk, close the Write window.

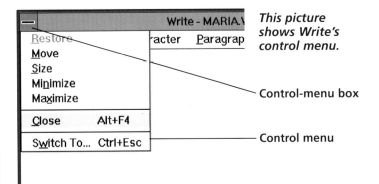

This picture shows Write's control menu.

Control-menu box

Control menu

Saving current changes

When you try to close a window, a box may appear on your screen telling you that you have changed your document since the last time you saved it. Your computer is checking whether or not you want to save the latest document version before you close its window.

If you want to save the current version of your document over the previous version, click the *Yes* button. If you don't want to save the current version, click *No*.

If you want to keep both the previous and current versions, click the *Cancel* button to return to your document, and use the *Save As...* command to save the current version under a new filename.

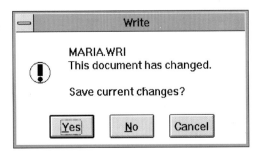

Write's "Save changes?" box

Paintbrush

This is the icon for Paintbrush, a Windows application which lets you create pictures on your screen. Use Program Manager to find and run the Paintbrush program. When the Paintbrush window appears on your desktop, maximize it so that you can take a closer look.

Picking a canvas size

The main area of the Paintbrush window shows a canvas on which you can create a picture. You can specify the size of the canvas you want to use, and choose whether you want your picture to be in colour or black and white. To do this, pick *Image Attributes...* from the *Options* menu. The dialog box shown below will appear:

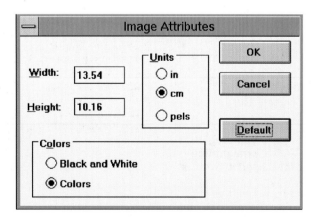

To set your canvas to a standard size, click on the *Default* button. If you want to paint with a variety of colours, make sure that the *Colors* option is selected. Then click the *OK* button.

Your canvas will now be slightly larger than the Paintbrush window's picture display area, so Paintbrush provides scroll bars to enable you to move your view across your canvas.

Choosing colours

Paintbrush provides several different drawing tools and a range of coloured paints to use them with.

To choose colours for your picture, you use the multicoloured strip at the bottom of the Paintbrush window. This is called the Palette.

Part of the Palette

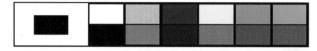

You can pick both a foreground colour to draw with, and a background colour to draw on. You will find out how each Paintbrush tool uses these two colours on the opposite page.

To pick a foreground colour, click on a colour in the Palette with the primary mouse button. To pick a background colour, click on a Palette colour with the secondary mouse button (see page 10). The box at the left-hand end of the Palette shows the colours you have chosen:

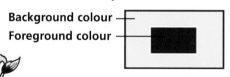

Background colour
Foreground colour

The Toolbox

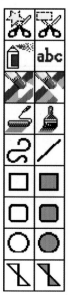

At the left-hand edge of the Paintbrush window is a panel of eighteen small pictures, called the Toolbox. You use the Toolbox to choose from Paintbrush's drawing tools, each of which creates a different effect on your canvas.

To select a tool, click on it in the Toolbox so that it is highlighted. You can then move it around the canvas using your mouse. Most tools appear in the picture area as a cross-shaped pointer, but some have their own particular pointer shape.

This is the Toolbox panel.

Special effects

The picture below shows some of the effects you can create using different drawing tools and colours. Have a go at producing your own Paintbrush work of art!

You can use the Brush tool like a crayon, dragging it to make a mark on the canvas in the foreground colour.

These tools let you drag out different shaped outlines. By holding down the Shift key as you use a tool, you can use the Ellipse tool to draw a perfect circle, or the Box tool to draw a perfect square. The outlines appear in the current foreground colour.

The Airbrush tool sprays the foreground colour onto the canvas as you drag it around.

Dragging the Eraser tool over part of your picture rubs it out by colouring over it in the background colour.

As you drag the Color Eraser across the canvas, it replaces any areas of the foreground colour with the background colour.

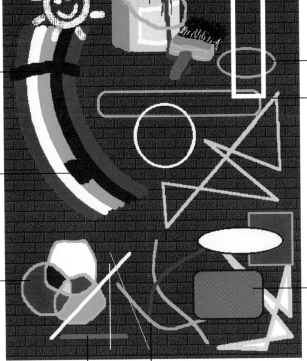

The Polygon tool lets you drag out a series of connected lines to create a many-sided shape called a polygon. The free end of the last line must join up with the free end of the first line to form a closed shape.

Clicking the Paint Roller tool inside an enclosed area fills in that area with the foreground colour.

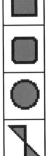

These tools let you drag out a filled-in shape. The border appears in the background colour, and the shape is filled in with the foreground colour.

The Line tool lets you draw a straight line. Drag the cross-shaped pointer from where you want the line to start, to where you want it to end. If you hold down the Shift key as you drag the Line tool you can draw vertical, horizontal and 45° diagonal lines.

This tool lets you drag out a straight line and then bend it twice, by dragging, to create a curve.

Changing your brush

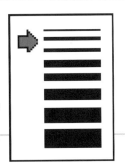

You can change the width of the Brush, Eraser, Color Eraser and Airbrush tools. Click on the width you want in the Linesize box in the bottom left-hand corner of the Paintbrush window. You can also use the Linesize box to set the thickness of curves, straight lines and the outlines of shapes.

The Linesize box

27

More about Paintbrush

Once you have drawn a Paintbrush picture, you can add text to it, or zoom in on part of it to add details. You can even cut bits out so that you can move or alter them.

Adding text

To add text to your picture, select the Text tool from the Toolbox.

As you move the pointer across the picture area, it will turn into an I-beam, like the one you used in Write. Position this I-beam where you want to add text to your picture, and click. An insertion point will appear, enabling you to type text onto your canvas in the current foreground colour.

The Text tool `abc`

Paintbrush styles

Like Write, Paintbrush lets you vary the appearance of text. You can use Paintbrush's *Text* menu to select a font and text size, or to pick the bold, italic or underline styles. Paintbrush also has two extra text style options. The *Outline* command produces foreground coloured text with a thin outline in the background colour. *Shadow* produces foreground coloured text with a shadow in the background colour.

The Outline style

The Shadow style

Changing your view

A standard Paintbrush window displays the Palette, the Toolbox, the Linesize box, and part of your canvas. But you can alter this standard view if you want.

If you pick *Zoom Out* from the *View* menu, Paintbrush displays your picture at a smaller scale, so that the entire canvas fits inside the picture area. You will find out on the opposite page why you may sometimes need to use this zoom out view. To return to the standard view, select *Zoom In* from the *View* menu.

To take a look at your picture without the Paintbrush controls around it, select the *View Picture* command from the *View* menu. To return to the controls, click anywhere on the display.

A Paintbrush window showing the standard view.

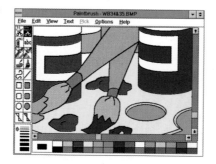

A Paintbrush window showing the Zoom Out view.

Zooming in close

You can work in detail on a small section of your picture by picking *Zoom In* from the *View* menu. Your pointer will change into a small rectangular box. Use your mouse to move this box over the section of your picture that you want to look at in detail, then click. The picture area will display a close-up of the selected section, showing the tiny squares, called pixels, which make up your picture.

You can alter the picture section one pixel at a time. Click the foreground colour into a pixel using the primary mouse button, or the background colour using the secondary mouse button.

When you have finished adding details to your picture section, select *Zoom Out* from the *View* menu to return to the standard Paintbrush view.

The Zoom In view

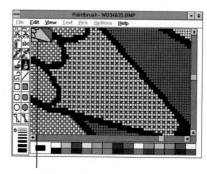

This box shows the picture section at actual size.

The cutout tools

The Toolbox includes two "cutout" tools. You use these to outline a section of your picture so that you can move it to a new position on your canvas, or alter it using the commands in Paintbrush's *Pick* menu.

These are the two cutout tools.

 The Scissor tool lets you draw a wavy outline to create an irregularly shaped cutout section.

 The Pick tool lets you drag out a rectangular outline to create a box-shaped cutout section.

Moving part of picture

Once you have cut out a section of your picture, you can drag it to a new position on your canvas. When the section is where you want it, click somewhere outside its outline and Paintbrush will place the section back on the canvas.

Alternatively, you can choose the *Cut* or *Copy* command from the *Edit* menu to place a cutout section on the Windows Clipboard. Pick *Paste*, and a copy of the cutout will appear in the top left-hand corner of the picture area. You can then drag the cutout section wherever you want on the canvas and click it into place.

WARNING!
When you click a cutout picture section into place, any part that doesn't fit within the picture display area is trimmed off. If you want to avoid this happening, select *Zoom Out* before you use a cutout tool. You can then use the Pick tool and the *Cut*, *Copy* and *Paste* commands to move cutout sections without damaging them.

Using the Pick menu

You can use the commands in Paintbrush's *Pick* menu to alter the appearance of parts of your picture. Use one of the cutout tools to outline the section you want to alter, then click on a *Pick* menu command.

This diagram shows what the Pick commands do.

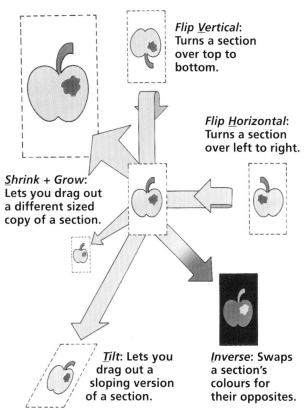

Flip Vertical: Turns a section over top to bottom.

Flip Horizontal: Turns a section over left to right.

Shrink + Grow: Lets you drag out a different sized copy of a section.

Tilt: Lets you drag out a sloping version of a section.

Inverse: Swaps a section's colours for their opposites.

Saving your artworks

You can keep a Paintbrush picture on disk just like any other Windows document. Use *Save As...* to store your picture in the root directory on the hard disk (see pages 22 and 23). Because you are saving a Paintbrush file, you need to use the Paintbrush filename extension, which is ".bmp". When you have completed and saved your picture, close Paintbrush's window.

Using File Manager

As you save more and more files on disk, it's important to keep track of where each one is stored. Windows has a program, called File Manager, which helps you do this.

Use Program Manager to find and run the File Manager program. It is usually found in a program group called Main. When the File Manager window opens on your desktop, maximize it to take a closer look.

This is File Manager's icon.

Avoiding accidents

File Manager lets you move files from one place to another on disk, change their filenames, or even delete them completely. You need to take care not to do any of these things by accident.

File Manager has a safety system to prevent accidental alterations. As soon as you open its window, check that this safety system is switched on. To do this, pick the *Confirmation...* command from the *Options* menu. Make sure that the dialog box which appears is filled in like the one below, with a cross in each of its five check boxes. Then click the *OK* button. File Manager will now ask for confirmation whenever you try to move, delete or alter a file.

File Manager's Confirmation box

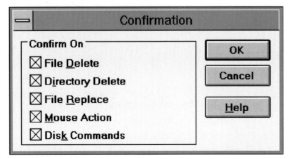

Tidying the display

To help you find your way around File Manager for the first time, it's a good idea to convert its window to a standard layout.

Hold down **Shift** and press the **F5** key. One or more windows will appear in a stack inside the File Manager window. These are called directory windows.

As a beginner, it's best to have only one directory window open at a time. So close all but one of the directory windows, using their control-menu boxes (see page 25).

Pick *Tree and Directory* from File Manager's *View* menu. This will divide the remaining directory window into two equal areas.

Your File Manager window will now look like this.

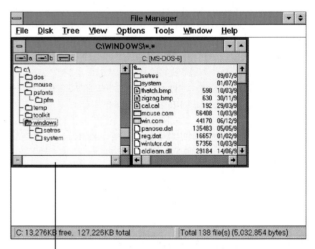

A directory window

Using a directory window

Files are grouped into separate directories on disk (see page 23). A File Manager directory window enables you to look inside a directory to see what files it holds.

It's possible to have several directory windows open inside File Manager, but only one of these windows can be active at a time. You can find out on the opposite page what the various parts of a directory window are used for.

The disk drive bar

Instead of a menu bar, a directory window has a bar containing several small symbols. Each symbol represents one of your computer's disk drives.

When you want to look at the contents of a particular disk, you select the drive which contains that disk by clicking on its symbol. Try clicking on the hard disk drive symbol (see page 23) to find out what files are stored on your hard disk.

A directory window disk drive bar

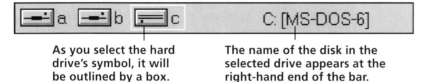

As you select the hard drive's symbol, it will be outlined by a box.

The name of the disk in the selected drive appears at the right-hand end of the bar.

The directory tree

The left-hand side of a directory window shows a diagram, called a directory tree. This represents the arrangement of directories on the disk inside the selected disk drive. Files grouped together in a directory are often separated again into further directories. The directories within a particular directory are known as its subdirectories. The directory tree diagram shows this arrangement as a series of folders inside other folders.

To take a closer look at the tree layout, select *Expand All* from File Manager's *Tree* menu, and use the scroll bar at the right-hand side of the directory tree to move your view to the top of the tree.

Roots and branches

Every disk has one main directory, called the root directory, which contains all the other directories on that disk. The root directory on the selected disk is represented by a folder symbol at the very top of the directory tree. Lines called branches run from the root directory symbol to other folder symbols, each representing a subdirectory inside the root directory. Some of these folders also have branches running to other folders, showing how they in turn are divided into subdirectories.

A directory tree

```
 c:\ ──────── root
               directory
 ├─ dos
 ├─ mouse
 ├─ psfonts
 │   └─ pfm
 ├─ temp
 ├─ toolkit
 └─ windows
     ├─ setres
     └─ system
```

Directory contents

You will find out on page 32 how to use the directory tree to find and select the directory that you want to look inside. Once a directory is selected in the tree, the right-hand side of the directory window shows a list of its contents.

A directory contents list

🔼...		▲
📁 setres		09/07/9
📁 system		01/07/9
📄 thatch.bmp	598	10/03/9
📄 zigzag.bmp	630	30/11/9
📄 cal.cal	192	29/03/9
🔲 mouse.com	56408	10/03/9
🔲 win.com	44170	06/12/9
📄 panose.dat	135483	05/05/9
📄 reg.dat	16657	01/02/9
📄 wintutor.dat	57356	10/03/9
📄 aldlearn.dll	29184	14/06/9 ▼

Paths

A directory window's title bar shows the "path" for the directory currently selected in the tree. This describes the route to the directory along the branches of the directory tree.

For example, if you wanted to look in the "system" directory inside the "windows" directory on the hard disk, you would need to open the hard disk root directory (labelled "c:"), open the "windows" directory inside that, and open the "system" directory inside that. The path for this directory would be written like this:

C:\WINDOWS\SYSTEM

Each step in the path is separated by a backslash (\).

Finding your files

Whenever you want to retrieve one of your Windows documents from disk, you can use File Manager to find and open its file.

Which disk?

To find a file, you first have to tell your computer which disk it is stored on. To do this, use the active directory window's disk drive bar, as described on page 31, to select the drive that holds the disk you want.

Picking a directory

Once you have selected a drive, the active directory window will display a directory tree for the disk inside it. Search this directory tree to find the directory in which your file is stored.

Sometimes the directory tree doesn't show the subdirectories contained within certain directories. You might have to alter the tree's layout so that it includes a separate folder symbol for the subdirectory that contains your file. This is known as expanding the directory tree.

Expanding branches

To expand the directory tree so that it shows a specific directory's subdirectories, select that directory by clicking on its folder symbol, and pick *Expand Branch* from File Manager's *Tree* menu. Alternatively, you can simply double-click on the directory's folder symbol. The directory's subdirectories will appear in the tree diagram.

The Windows directory before and after it is expanded

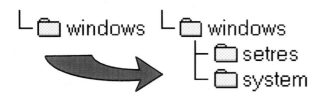

Expanding tips

To help you remember which directories contain subdirectories, make sure there is a tick next to *Indicate Expandable Branches* in File Manager's *Tree* menu. A small "+" sign will appear inside the folder symbol of any directory that contains subdirectories which are not shown in the tree.

The easiest way to ensure that the directory tree displays the entire layout of directories and subdirectories, showing a separate folder symbol for each one, is to pick *Expand All* from File Manager's *Tree* menu.

The contents list

When you have found the directory containing your file, click on its folder symbol to open it up. A list of the directory's contents will appear in the right-hand half of the directory window.

The directory contents list

Each of your document files is represented by this symbol

setres		09/07/9
system		01/07/9
thatch.bmp	598	10/03/9
zigzag.bmp	630	30/11/9
cal.cal	192	29/03/9
mouse.com	56408	10/03/9
win.com	44170	06/12/9
panose.dat	135483	05/05/9
reg.dat	16657	01/02/9
wintutor.dat	57356	10/03/9
aldlearn.dll	29184	14/06/9

Opening a file

Use the scroll bar at the right-hand edge of the directory window to look through the directory contents list. When you find the file you want, open it by clicking on its filename so that it is highlighted, and picking the *Open* command from File Manager's *File* menu. Alternatively, you can simply double-click on its filename.

As you open the file, the window of the application that you used to create it will appear on your desktop, containing your document.

Finding lost files

The instructions on the opposite page only enable you to find and open a file if you can remember where it is stored. If you've forgotten where the file you want is kept, you'll need to use File Manager's *Search...* command to track it down.

The Search box

To find a lost file, you first have to tell your computer which part of which disk you want it to search. If you can remember which directory the file you want is in, use File Manager's active directory window to find and select it. If you can't remember, select the root directory so that your computer will search the entire disk.

Once you have selected a directory, pick *Search...* from File Manager's *File* menu. The Search dialog box will appear on your desktop.

File Manager's Search dialog box

Search		
Search For:	*.*	OK
Start From:	C:\	Cancel
☒ Search All Subdirectories		Help

Specifying a search range

The "Start From" box inside the Search dialog box shows the path for the directory you are about to search (see page 31). If you decide that you want your computer to search a different directory from the one currently selected in the tree, type the alternative directory's path in the Start From box.

Make sure that there is a cross in the "Search all subdirectories" check box. This ensures that your computer will look through all the subdirectories of the directory that you've named.

Entering a search name

The "Search For" box inside the Search dialog box lets you type in the name of the file that you're looking for. If you can't remember the exact filename, you can enter an approximate version. Substitute a "*" character in the place of any part of the name that you've forgotten. Your computer will try to find a filename which matches your approximation.

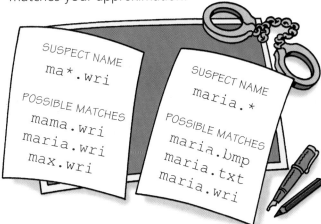

Search results

Once you have entered a search range and name, click the *OK* button to start your search. File Manager will track down all the files inside the search range with filenames that match your Search For name.

A window will appear inside the File Manager window, listing the names of any files which match your search details. If you can see the file you are looking for in the Results window, you can open it up by selecting it and picking *Open* from the *File* menu, or by double-clicking on its name.

The Search Results window

Search Results: C:\ma*.wri				
🗎 c:\maria.wri	512	22/11/95	11:44:56	a

Organizing your files

If you want to rearrange your files on disk, you can use File Manager to move them about. These pages tell you how to use the active directory window to organize your files.

Your own directory

The best way of organizing your files so that they are easy to find is to create a directory of your own to keep them in. Have a go at creating a personal directory on your computer's hard disk. Select the hard disk root directory in the directory tree, and pick *Create Directory...* from File Manager's *File* menu. A dialog box will appear, enabling you to type in a name for your new directory. As with filenames, directory names can only have eight characters, and cannot include spaces, or any of the characters shown below:

.:/\[]*|<>+=;,?

When you have entered a directory name, click the *OK* button. Your new personal directory will appear in the tree, as a subdirectory of the hard disk root directory. You can store all your future files inside this directory by selecting it whenever you use a Save As box (see pages 22 and 23).

Source to destination

You can use File Manager to move a file from one directory to another on a disk. To do this, use the active directory window to take the file from its original disk location, known as its source, and put it in a new location, known as its destination. The diagram below shows how you use the active directory window to move a file.

Moving a file

1. Make sure the destination directory is displayed in the directory tree. Expand the tree if necessary.

2. Open the source directory and find the file that you want to move in the directory contents list.

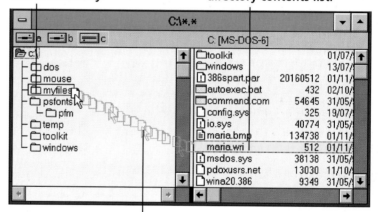

3. Drag the file across onto the folder symbol of the destination directory. As you drag a file it appears as a small document symbol.

4. When the document symbol is correctly positioned over the destination directory, the directory is outlined by a box. Release the mouse button.

Try moving the Write letter file that you saved on page 23, and the Paintbrush picture file that you saved on page 29, into your own directory on your computer's hard disk.

Copying a file

You can create a copy of a file and put it in another directory without removing the original from its source directory. To do this, follow the same procedure as for moving a file, but hold down the **Ctrl** key as you drag the file into the destination directory. This will leave a copy of the file in both the source and destination directories.

Disk to disk

File Manager even lets you transfer a file from one disk to another. This is useful if you want to copy a file from your hard disk onto a floppy disk, so that you can move it to another PC.

To copy a file from one disk to another, you first have to open up the directory you want to copy the file into. Use File Manager's active directory window to open this directory on the destination disk.

Next use the directory window to look for the file that you want to copy on the source disk. When you find the file, drag it onto the disk drive bar. Position it over the symbol of the drive which contains the destination disk, and release the mouse button.

Copying a file to a different disk

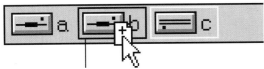

When the file is positioned correctly, a black box will outline the destination drive's symbol.

To move a file from one disk to another, rather than copy it, hold down the **Shift** key as you drag the file onto the destination drive's symbol.

Using Re**n**ame

If you decide that you want to change the name of a file or directory, use the active directory window to find and select it. Then pick *Rena̲me...* from File Manager's *Fi̲le* menu. Use the dialog box that appears on your desktop to enter a new name, and click *OK*.

Deleting files

If you want to get rid of a file completely, use the active directory window to find and select it. Then pick *Delete* from the *Fi̲le* menu.

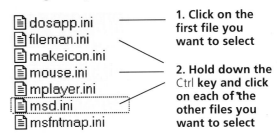

Multiple selection

File Manager lets you handle several files at once. To do this, you need to select the files from the directory contents list, using the multiple selection technique shown below.

Selecting multiple files

dosapp.ini	—— 1. Click on the first file you want to select
fileman.ini	
makeicon.ini	
mouse.ini	—— 2. Hold down the Ctrl key and click on each of the other files you want to select
mplayer.ini	
msd.ini	
msfntmap.ini	

Once you have selected them, you can move, copy or delete multiple files using the same techniques as you would for an individual file.

WARNING!

Each time you move, copy or delete files, a box will appear on your desktop asking you to confirm your command. Always check the details in this box before you give File Manager the go-ahead by clicking *Ye̲s*.

A typical File Manager confirmation box

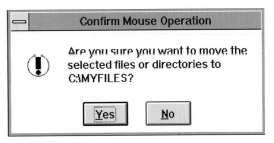

Never delete, move, or rename any files other than your own. They may be essential to your computer's proper functioning, or important to another user.

Printing a document

Once you have created a Windows document, you can use a printer to produce a copy of it on paper.

On and On-line

Before you try to print a document, make sure that your printer is plugged in, connected to your computer, and switched on. You also need to check that the printer is "on-line", which means that it is ready to receive information from your PC. Usually you press an on-line button on the printer. A light comes on to show you that the printer is on-line.

The Print box

Windows applications have a Print dialog box, which lets you give your PC the information it needs to print your document properly.

Have a go at printing out the letter that you created on pages 16 to 21. Open the Write window and open your letter file. Select the *Print...* command from Write's *File* menu. Write's Print box, shown below, will appear:

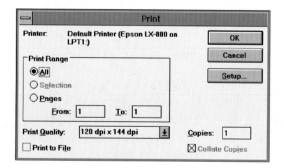

How many copies?

The *Copies* setting inside a Print box lets you tell your computer how many copies of your document you want. To print a single copy of your letter, type "1" in the *Copies* setting box.

Which pages?

If your document has several pages, the *Print Range* setting lets you specify which of these pages you want to print. To print your entire letter, select *All* in the *Print Range* setting box.

You are now ready to start printing. Click the *OK* button. The Print dialog box will vanish and a smaller box will appear on your desktop, confirming that your document is being printed.

Printing problems

Your computer may be set up so that Windows automatically runs a special program called Print Manager whenever you print a document. If anything goes wrong with the print-out, Print Manager displays a message on your desktop, advising you what to do to overcome the printing problem.

If you have difficulties printing your document, and Print Manager fails to help, run through the following check list:

1- Is your printer plugged in and connected to the computer correctly?

2- Is the printer switched on and on-line?

3- Have you put paper in the printer?

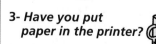

4- Is your computer set up to use this kind of printer? Does the printer you are using match the one named in the Print dialog box?

Exploring applications

By working with Write and Paintbrush, you have come across the main parts of the Windows system and used all the standard Windows techniques. You can now use what you have learned to explore other Windows applications on your computer.

Finding your way around

Approach unfamiliar applications step-by-step, using the techniques described in this book. If you need a reminder of how to perform a particular task, flick to the relevant page to refresh your memory. You could start your explorations by trying out the Windows application called Notepad.

This noticeboard shows how you can apply what you know to approach Notepad for the first time.

① Find and run the Notepad program using Program Manager.
Pages 14&15

② Use the Notepad window on your desktop to create a text document.
Pages 16&17

③ Edit your document using menu commands and dialog boxes.
Pages 18-21

④ If you want a copy of your Notepad notes on paper, use a printer to print them out.
Page 36

⑤ When you have finished with Notepad, save your notes as a file on disk, and close the Notepad window.
Pages 22-25

⑥ Use File Manager if you want to move, copy, or rename your Notepad files.
Pages 30-35

HELP!
As you explore a new application, make use of the instructions included in the Windows Help system. You can find out how to use these Help instructions on pages 44 and 45.

Not quite Write

Some applications will seem very different from the ones you've used so far. They won't look much like Write or Paintbrush, and might be used for other things than creating documents. But you can still use your mouse skills to control these applications on your desktop, and your experience of menus and dialog boxes to explore what they can do.

For an example of a very different kind of Windows application, try out a program called Solitaire, included in the Games program group. Solitaire's window lets you play a solo card-game on your Windows desktop.

The Solitaire window

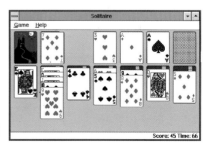

Windows gadgets

These pages introduce some of the other handy applications included in the standard Windows software.

Use the approach described on the previous page to explore each of these applications. They are usually found in a program group called Accessories.

Calculator

 The Windows Calculator is useful if you have any sums to do. You operate it just like an ordinary calculator, using the pointer to click on its buttons.

Calculator looks like this.

Calculator				▼
Edit **View** **Help**				

				0.
C	CE	Back		
MC	7	8	9	/	sqrt
MR	4	5	6	*	%
MS	1	2	3	-	1/x
M+	0	+/-	.	+	=

If you pick the *Scientific* command from the *View* menu, lots of extra buttons appear. You can use these if you need to carry out more complicated calculations.

Notepad

 Notepad enables you to jot down lists, reminders, or other straightforward text documents. You type your text onto a page within a window, using an I-beam and insertion point system just like Write's. Unlike Write, however, Notepad has only one font, and few editing options.

By choosing *Word Wrap* from Notepad's *Edit* menu, you can make sure that your text always fits within the window's side borders, as it does in the picture below.

This is a Notepad window.

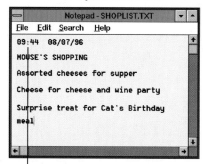

To stamp the date and time in your notes, press the F5 **key.**

If you want to save your notes as a file on disk, remember to use the Notepad filename extension, ".txt". To print out your shopping list or memo, pick *Print* from Notepad's *File* menu.

Clock

 The Clock application displays a clock-face inside a window on your desktop. You can make this clock-face as large or small as you like by changing the size of Clock's window. The *Settings* menu lets you choose between a clock-face with hands (analog) or with numbers (digital).

The analog clock-face

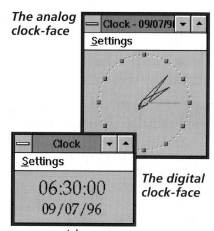

The digital clock-face

To pick a font for the digital clock-face, use the *Set Font...* command in Clock's *Settings* menu. If you want to hide the Clock window's title and menu bars, pick *No Title* from the *Settings* menu. To display them again, double-click anywhere on the clock-face.

You can choose to have the Clock window permanently on top of your desktop. To do this, pick *Always on Top* from Clock's control menu.

Calendar

 This application lets you create your own Windows calendar. When you first open the Calendar window, it shows a blank page listing the hours of the day. To add a reminder or appointment, simply type it onto this blank schedule. You can use arrow buttons beneath Calendar's menu bar to flick through similar schedules for other dates.

Calendar's daily view

If you press the **F9** key, Calendar will display a monthly calendar. Use the arrow buttons to flick backwards or forwards through the months of the year. You can mark a particular date for special attention by clicking on it and then picking the _Mark..._ command from the _Options_ menu. If you double-click on a date, Calendar displays the schedule for that day.

Calendar's monthly view

You can create separate calendars for your home, school or work schedule, for birthdays, or for other important events. Save each calendar as a separate file on disk using the filename extension ".cal".

Cardfile

 Cardfile lets you store information on an alphabetically ordered set of cards. It is ideal for noting down addresses, telephone numbers, or similar details.

To add a new card to a cardfile, press **F7**. A dialog box will appear asking you to enter an "index line" for the new card. This is the title by which the card will be alphabetically sorted. For instance, if you were creating a cardfile of friends' addresses, each card would have a friend's name as an index line.

Once you have typed in an index line for your new card, it will be slotted into its alphabetical position in your cardfile. You can then type whatever information you like onto the card.

This Cardfile window shows a sample address file.

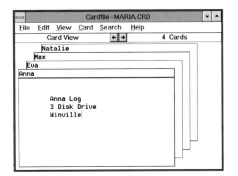

You can create as many cardfiles as you like. Save each one as a separate file on disk, using the filename extension ".crd". When you want to look at the information stored in one of your cardfiles, use the _Open..._ command in Cardfile's _File_ menu to retrieve it from disk.

To find a particular card, use the arrow buttons beneath the window's menu bar to flick through your cardfile. Alternatively, you can use the _Go To..._ command in Cardfile's _Search_ menu to specify the index line of the card that you want to look at. Cardfile will then retrieve the card automatically.

The _Print_ command in Cardfile's _File_ menu lets you print out one or all of the cards in a cardfile, so that you can have a copy of the stored information on paper.

Organizing your desktop

Windows lets you have several programs on your desktop at the same time. These pages tell you how to organize your desktop as it becomes crowded with windows and icons.

Switching

There are all sorts of occasions when you need to run several programs. For example, if you were writing a story using Write, you might want to open a Paintbrush window to create illustrations for your story. You might also want to look in your Windows Notepad (see page 38) to find plot ideas that you jotted down earlier.

This screen shows a busy desktop.

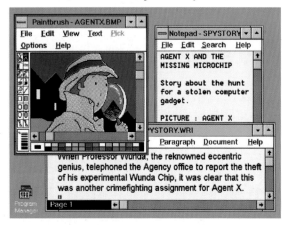

As your desktop becomes crowded with windows and icons, it gets harder to find the program that you want to use next. You need to bring that program's window to the top of the desktop. This is known as switching.

Usually you can switch to a program by clicking on part of its window or, if it is running in minimized form, by double-clicking on its icon. But if you can't see either the program's window or its icon, you'll need to use one of the following special switching techniques.

Using Alt+Tab

The first way of switching to a program which is running, but which you can't find on your desktop, is to use the **Alt** and **Tab** keys. Hold down the **Alt** key and press the **Tab** key. A box will appear in the middle of your screen showing the icon and name of a running program.

The Alt+Tab switching box

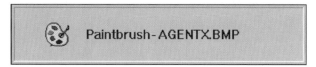

Keep **Alt** held down and press **Tab** repeatedly. Each of the programs that are running will appear in the box in turn. When the icon and name of the program you want appear, release the **Alt** key, and the selected program's window will jump to the top of the desktop.

The Task List

The second way of switching to a hidden program is to use a box known as the Task List. Hold down the **Ctrl** key and press the **Esc** key. Release both keys and the Task List box will appear on your desktop.

The Task List box

The Task List shows a list of all the programs currently running on your desktop. You can look through this list and highlight the program that you want to use by clicking on its name. Click on the Task List's *Switch To* button to bring this program's window to the top of your desktop.

Cascade and Tile

The Task List box contains several other useful buttons. Clicking the _Cascade_ button gathers all the windows that are currently open into a tidy pile in the middle of your desktop. The active window lies on top of the pile. Clicking the _Tile_ button changes the size of all open windows so that they fit neatly next to one another on your desktop.

Using either _Cascade_ or _Tile_ creates a space at the bottom of the display for the icons of any programs that are running in minimized form. If these icons become scattered around your desktop, you can line them up neatly by clicking the _Arrange Icons_ button in the Task List box.

Cascaded windows

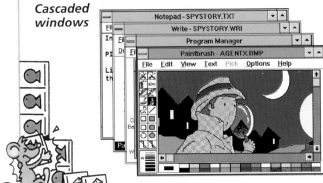

Tiled windows

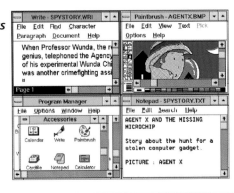

Clearing up

The more programs you have running, the slower your computer will work. So it's a good idea to close programs that you have finished with.

You can find out on page 25 how to close a window using its control-menu box. To close a program which is running in minimized form, click on its icon. The program's control menu will appear. Click on _Close_. The program will stop running and vanish from the desktop.

You can also use the Task List to clear away programs. Call up the Task List, select the name of the program that you want to close, and click on the _End Task_ button.

The ideal layout

Controlling several programs is easiest if you have only one program's window open at a time. All the other programs should be running in minimized form, lined up as icons along the bottom edge of the desktop.

To set up this layout, minimize all but one of the windows on your desktop. Then call up the Task List and click on its _Tile_ button. This desktop layout gives you plenty of room in the window you are using. It also lets you switch quickly to other running programs when you need to.

To switch from one program to another, simply minimize the window on screen and double-click on the icon of the program you want to use next. Then use the _Tile_ button to make the new active window a convenient size.

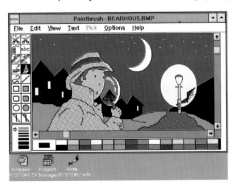

This screen shows the ideal desktop layout.

Combining applications

Windows lets you move information from one document to another. You can even combine information created by different applications. As an example of this, these pages show you how to combine Paintbrush and Write to produce an illustrated text document.

Transferring information with Clipboard

The simplest way to combine Windows applications is to use the Clipboard, introduced on page 19, to transfer information between them.

Try inserting a Paintbrush picture in the Write document that you produced on pages 16 to 21. To do this, first use Paintbrush to produce an illustration for your letter. When you've finished your drawing, use the Pick or Scissor tool to cut it out (see page 29). Copy this cutout onto the Clipboard by picking *Copy* from Paintbrush's *Edit* menu. Then save your picture, as described on pages 22 and 23, and close Paintbrush's window.

The Clipboard now holds a copy of your Paintbrush picture. To insert it in your letter, open your Write file (see page 24). Position the insertion point where you want the illustration to appear in your letter. Pick *Paste* from Write's *Edit* menu. Your Paintbrush picture will be copied from the Clipboard into your document.

Pictures and text cannot appear on the same line in a Write document. The text of your letter will split so that it fits above and below the inserted Paintbrush picture.

This diagram shows how you can use Clipboard to move information from one application to another.

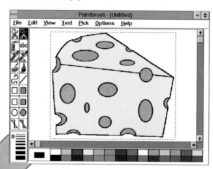

*1. Select the information you want to move, and use the **C**opy command to place it on the Clipboard.*

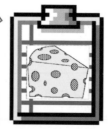

*2. Open the document in which you want to insert the information, and use **P**aste to copy it off the Clipboard.*

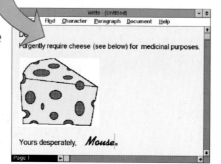

Moving a picture

Once you've inserted a picture in your Write letter, you can change its position so that your combined document looks just the way you want it to.

To move your picture to the left or right in your document, first select it by clicking on it with the I-beam. Then pick the *Move Picture* command from Write's *Edit* menu. A square pointer will appear near the middle of the inserted picture.

Write's special square pointer

By moving the square pointer with your mouse, you can shift your picture's outline across your document. Position the outline where you want the picture to be. Then click, and the picture will be moved to this new location.

To move your picture to a completely different place in your Write document, select it with the I-beam, and place it back on the Clipboard using the *Cut* command. You can then use the insertion point and *Paste* command to insert the picture wherever you want in your document.

What size?

If you want to alter the size of your inserted picture, use the I-beam to select it, and pick the *Size Picture* command from Write's *Edit* menu. The square pointer will appear again. This time, you can use it to stretch or shrink your picture.

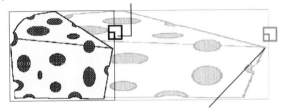

Resizing an inserted picture

As you move the square pointer over one of the picture's borderlines, it will grab that borderline.

Move the borderline to the position you want. Then click to make the picture appear at this size.

Editing your picture

You might want to alter your picture after you have inserted it in your letter. To do this, select the picture with the I-beam and pick *Edit Paintbrush Picture Object* from Write's *Edit* menu. Alternatively, you can simply double-click on the picture with the I-beam.

A Paintbrush window containing your picture will appear. Use the Paintbrush controls to make any alterations. When you have finished, pick the *Update* command from the Paintbrush window's *File* menu. This tells your computer to replace the copy of the picture in your Write document with the altered version. Pick *Exit & Return to...* from the Paintbrush window's *File* menu to return to your document.

Saving a combined document

When you have finished your illustrated letter, use Write's Save As box to save it as a file on disk. Keep it with your other documents in the personal hard disk directory that you created on page 34. Because you have combined your letter and picture inside the Write window, use Write's filename extension, ".wri".

Other combinations

You can combine many of the other applications on your PC in much the same way as Write and Paintbrush. You could try using the Clipboard to insert Notepad notes into a Calendar schedule, or to move Paintbrush pictures into a Cardfile to produce an illustrated address book.

If your PC has extra application software for creating sounds or animation, you can even insert noises and moving pictures into your Windows documents.

HELP!

You can use an application's Help system to find out how to insert information created by other applications. Pages 44 and 45 explain how to use the Windows Help system.

How to get help

Windows includes its own set of instructions, called the Help system. As you explore an application, you can use the information in the Help system to tackle unfamiliar commands and controls, or to remind yourself of specific Windows techniques.

Calling for Help

To get help with a particular program, you have to make sure that its window is active. Then either press and release the **F1** key, or pick the *Contents* command from the program's *Help* menu. A Help window showing the program's Help Contents page will appear on your desktop.

This is the Contents page for Write's Help system.

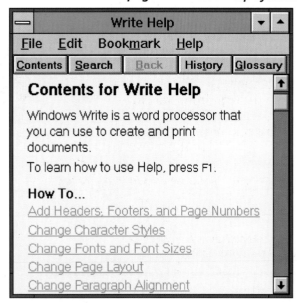

Help topics

Each program's Help instructions are organized into separate topics, as in an instruction manual. The Help Contents page lists these topics, showing each one as an underlined title. Use the scroll bar to look through the Contents list and find a topic which sounds as if it will cover the information you need.

Choosing a topic

Once you have found the topic you want, point at its title in the Contents list. The pointer will turn into a hand shape like this:

By clicking on a topic title with the hand-shaped pointer, you can jump to the Help section which explains that topic. Whenever you want to return to the Help Contents page to choose a new topic, click on the *Contents* button at the top of the Help window.

The **S**earch button

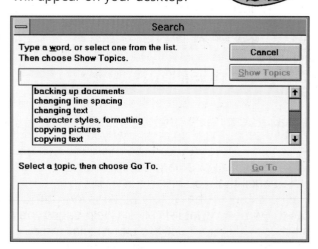

Another way of finding information on a specific topic, is to use the Search option. Click on the Help window's *Search* button and the dialog box below will appear on your desktop:

Follow the instructions in the upper half of the Search box to specify the subject about which you need information. You can type it in, or scroll through the list of available subjects to find and highlight the one you want.

Once you have specified a subject, click on the *Show Topics* button. All the Help topics relating to your chosen subject will appear in a list in the lower half of the Search box. Highlight the topic you want by clicking on it, then click on the *Go To* button to jump to that Help topic.

The Glossary

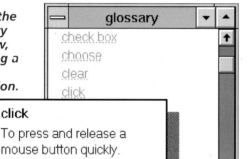

Some of the more difficult computer words included in the Help instructions are underlined with a line of dashes. If you click the hand-shaped pointer on any of these words, a small box will appear containing a brief explanation of what that word means.

By clicking on the *Glossary* button you can browse through a list of all these tricky computer words in a window on your desktop. Click the hand-shaped pointer on any word in the Glossary window to find out what it means.

This is the Glossary window, showing a sample definition.

glossary
check box
choose
clear
click

click

To press and release a mouse button quickly.

Back and **H**istory

Clicking on the *Back* button in a Help window takes you back to the Help page that you were using last. You can use this button to go back one page at a time through the Help pages that you have already used.

By clicking on the *History* button, you can open a window that lists all the Help pages you have used. To jump back to a particular topic, double-click on its title in the History list.

This is the Windows Help History window.

Windows Help History
Inserting Drawings
Contents for Write Help
Changing Page Layout
Contents for Write Help
Changing Character Styles
Contents for Write Help

The topics are listed in the order in which you looked at them, with the most recent last.

HELP!

You can even use Help to find out how to use Help. Pick the *How to Use Help* command from the *Help* menu, or press the **F1** key twice in succession.

The Windows Tutorial

As well as the Help system, Windows includes a two-part lesson called the Windows Tutorial. The first part helps you learn the main mouse techniques (see page 11). The second part of the Tutorial, called Windows Basics, covers the skills introduced on pages 8 to 20 of this book.

To find the Tutorial, switch to Program Manager's window and pick *Windows Tutorial* from its *Help* menu. Press the **w** key to select Windows Basics.

You don't have to follow the lesson through from start to finish. You can flick backwards or forwards through its pages using the buttons at the bottom right-hand corner of the screen. By clicking on the *Contents* button, you can display the Tutorial Contents page and use a Topic button to jump to a particular section of the lesson.

This screen shows the Windows Tutorial Contents Page.

Contents

Click the button for the topic you want to learn about.

	Windows Basics Lessons
Begin the Tutorial again	Instructions
Exit the Tutorial	Starting an Application
	Moving and Sizing Windows
Mouse Lesson	Using Menus and Commands
Begin Mouse Lesson	Using Dialog Boxes
	Switching Between Applications
	Closing Applications

Return to the Tutorial   To return to your current location in the Tutorial

45

Introducing Windows 95

Microsoft has developed a new operating system, called Windows 95. It is designed to be easier to use than earlier Windows software, and to enable PC users to take full advantage of advances in computer technology.

Windows 95 plays the same role as previous versions of Windows. It allows you to control your PC using a mouse pointer and pictures on your screen. Windows, icons, menus and dialog boxes all appear on the Windows 95 desktop.

However, there are several important ways in which Windows 95 differs from earlier Windows software.

The Start button

Program Manager is replaced in the Windows 95 system by a single button on the desktop, called the Start buttton.

By clicking on the Start button, you can open a menu that lists every program available on your computer. You can use this Start button menu to find and run the programs you want to use.

The Start button

The Taskbar

The Start button is found at one end of a narrow strip, called the Taskbar. The Taskbar can be positioned along any edge of the Windows 95 desktop. It is never hidden from view by other desktop items.

In addition to the Start button, the Taskbar includes a button for each program that your computer is currently running. By clicking a program's button on the Taskbar, you can bring that program's window to the top of the desktop. This provides a quick and easy way to switch between windows.

Part of the Taskbar

🎬 Start	🖥 Control Panel	💿 CD Player

New gadgets

The Windows 95 desktop includes several new helpful gadgets, some of which you can see on the desktop on the right.

A Windows 95 desktop.

Double-clicking on the My Computer icon opens a window displaying all your computer's disk drives and devices. This makes it easy to select the part of your PC's system that you want to use.

By dragging a file onto this icon, you can put it in the Recycle Bin. If you need the file later on, you can open the Recycle Bin window and retrieve it. Emptying the Bin, deletes all the files inside it from disk.

My Briefcase automatically gathers together the programs and documents that you use most often. By opening the My Briefcase window, you can find these frequently used items quickly and easily.

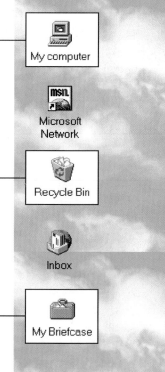

A new filing system

File Manager is replaced in Windows 95 by a new filing system. Two separate programs, called File Find and Explorer, enable you to track down files, or reorganize them on disk.

Windows 95 filenames can be as long as you like. You don't need to add extensions to them (see page 22) because Windows 95 works out for itself which application was used to create each file.

Phileas File-Filington III Jnr.

Multitasking

Windows 95 enables your computer to do several different jobs at the same time. This is called multitasking. It means that you don't have to wait for your computer to finish one job before starting work on another.

The desktop below shows an example of multitasking. The user is playing cards with one program, while another program copies files.

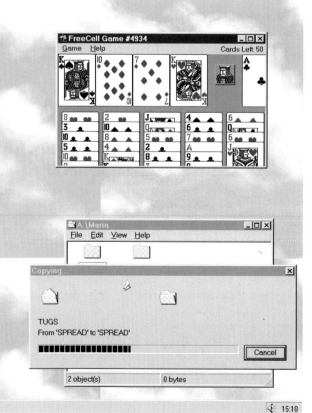

Multimedia advances

"Multimedia" means using a computer to combine text, sound, pictures and video to present information.

Advances in computer technology mean that PCs are becoming better and better at handling multimedia.

The Windows 95 system is designed so that you can work with different kinds of information easily and effectively. It enables you to use your PC to run existing multimedia "presentations", or even to create your own.

Joining the network

A group of computers linked together so that they can exchange information is called a network.

PCs can be connected with other PCs nearby to form a local area network. They can even be connected over long distances, via the telephone system, to form a wide area network. Some wide area computer networks stretch all the way around the world.

Windows 95 has several features to help you use networks. The Network Neighborhood program enables your PC to function as part of a local area network. Another program, called The Microsoft Network, lets you join and use Microsoft's own international PC network.

All the information that your computer has recently received from the network is gathered together in the "Inbox" on the Windows 95 desktop.

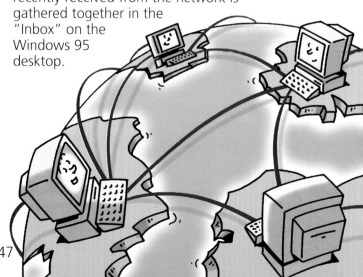

Index

First published in 1996 by Usborne Publishing Ltd, Usborne House, 83-85 Saffron Hill London EC1N 8RT, England. Copyright © 1996 Usborne Publishing Ltd. The name Usborne and the device 🌂 are Trade Marks of Usborne Publishing Ltd. All rights reserved. No part of this publication may be reproduced, stored in a retrieval system or transmitted in any form or by any means, electronic, mechanical, photocopying, recording or otherwise, without the prior permission of the publisher.
First published in America in August 1996. Printed in Spain.